RUSTY RACCOON

and The Sugar Bowl

ETHAN & SHERRY LUHMAN

Illustrated by Sherry Luhman

THIS BOOK BELONGS TO:

_____

Published by Orange Hat Publishing 2020
ISBN 978-1-64538-177-8

For information, please contact:

Orange Hat Publishing
www.orangehatpublishing.com
Waukesha, WI

Photography Credit: Lauren Conant | Ren Colleen Photography
website: https://www.rencolleen.com/

Writing a children's book has been a dream of ours for quite some time, and it has been a joy to see Rusty Raccoon come to life. Beginning as a bedtime story for our children, this book is first and foremost dedicated to them. Because of their adventurous spirits and love for the outdoors + animals, this book exists. We have spent countless hours cuddled up reading as a family, and it is time together that we will always cherish.

We also dedicate this book to Grandpa Gary and Uncle Dave. We miss them every day, and we know that their memory will live on in these pages. We want our children to know their storytelling and sense of humor, and the characters you'll meet do just that.

May Rusty Raccoon and the Sugar Bowl take you on an adventure together full of life's timeless joys alongside the company of loyal friends and loving family. We hope this book means as much to you as it does to us.

All of our love,
Ethan & Sherry Luhman + our little tribe

Every year, Rusty Raccoon and his family went to a black raspberry patch. It was tucked away deep in the woods, where no one else, other than a sneaky little raccoon, could find it. This black raspberry patch had the biggest, sweetest, juiciest raspberries you've ever tasted. That's why it was called The Sugar Bowl.

Now, you might like black raspberries. You might like how sweet and juicy they are, with just a hint of sour and tartness. Or you might not like black raspberries, because of all the seeds and little hairs that grow on them. But whether you like them or not, you would love the black raspberries from The Sugar Bowl. They were like Mother Nature's candy, and there was nothing sweeter anywhere in Oarwood Forest.

Leaf

Fruit

Stem

WILD BLACK RASPBERRY

Rubus Occidentalis

This year, Rusty Raccoon wanted to take his friends Dave Deer, Winston Squirrel, and Gary Bear to The Sugar Bowl. And he was pretty sure he knew how to get there. Rusty's dad led their family to The Sugar Bowl every year. It was a tradition Rusty's grandpa had started when his dad was a little kid. So Rusty went to find his dad.

"Dad, I want to take my friends to eat the best black raspberries at The Sugar Bowl. Can I, please?"

"That's a great idea! Rusty, I think you're ready to lead the way on your own, but are you sure you remember how to get there?" his dad asked.

"Well, I'm pretty sure," Rusty responded, feeling confident his feet would remember the way, if only he could just get going.

"Let's go over the directions, because The Sugar Bowl is trickier to find than you might think. And if you miss it, you'll end up in one of two places.

"You'll either end up in The Briar Patch (and those are the yuckiest blackberries you'll ever lay your paws on!), or right smack-dab in The Coyote Den. And then you won't be finding a snack... you'll *be* the snack!"

That did not sound good at all. But Rusty was not worried. He had been to The Sugar Bowl many times.

"Yeah, yeah, Dad. You tell us that story *every* year about your brother getting his tail bit off trying to sneak past a coyote. Just keep going."

His dad gave him a look.

"*Please*, can you keep going?" Rusty pleaded.

"Okay, listen closely, Rusty. First, you'll go straight north out of our home and take a left at the stand of red pines. Second, you'll walk through a meadow, and you will see the biggest white oak tree you've ever seen. That's where we always stop for those delicious wild turnips and a few acorns, remember? One time, I stumbled upon a whole bunch of-"

"I know, a whole bunch of dried apples some animal forgot about," Rusty interrupted.

"Uh-hmm . . . Yes. That's right. Third, you circle along the oak until you find the spot with the twisted knot. Fourth, go straight up the hill right in front of the twisted knot. When you get to the top of that hill, you'll look down and see the Red River. But don't go toward the Red River. Instead, go toward where the sun sets in the summer sky. Finally, you'll see a rock. Not too big and not too small, and on the other side of that rock, there's The Sugar Bowl."

"Okay Dad, I pretty much remember it all from last year. First, I'll head north to the stand of red pines, and then through the meadow until I see the um, the ummmm…"

"The BIGGEST white oak tree you've ever seen," his dad added.

"Yes! Biggest white oak, I was just about to say that!" Rusty exclaimed. "Then I look for the twisted knot and head straight up the hill and look for the Red River. But I don't head toward the Red River, I head toward where the sun sets in the summer sky. See, I'm ready!"

"Well, what about the rock?" asked his dad.

"Of course! I know, not too big, not too small, and The Sugar Bowl is right on the other side! Got it. Can we go now?"

His dad nodded.

"Thanks, Dad!" With that Rusty set off with his friends to begin their adventure.

"Have fun, Rusty," his dad called after him.

"Follow me, friends! I know exactly how to get there. Just wait until you taste those black raspberries!"

As they walked and talked, Rusty saw the tall red pine trees. *Do we go left or right?* Rusty wondered. "I think we go left," he said as he tried to remember what came next. *I should have paid more attention.*

Rusty saw a meadow straight ahead, and then he knew they were going the right way. They kept walking through the meadow, when suddenly Rusty saw a huge oak tree, like a giant tent in the middle of the meadow.

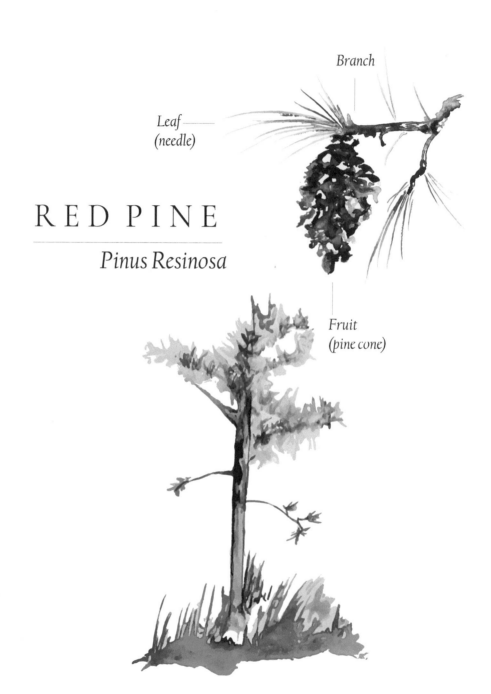

Branch

Leaf
(needle)

RED PINE

Pinus Resinosa

Fruit
(pine cone)

Leaf

Fruit
(acorn)

Branch

WHITE OAK

Quercus Alba

"Straight up this hill now!" Rusty said confidently.

"My stomach is grumbling. Can we stop and eat some acorns?" Winston Squirrel asked.

"Yeah, I want a snack," Gary Bear agreed. "I'm hungry."

"You two are always hungry!" Dave Deer said.

"Let's keep moving," Rusty said, "just wait till we get there. You'll be happy we didn't stop for silly acorns."

"Fine. Next stop—The Sugar Bowl!" Winston said.

They started walking up the hill but missed the twisted knot.

Rusty knew what was next: at the top of this hill, he would look down and see the Red River. But when they got to the top of the hill, the Red River was nowhere to be found!

Oh, no, he thought, *I forgot something*. He thought and thought and thought, and he twisted his face all around. But he couldn't remember. *Well*, he reasoned, *maybe it's just because the trees are taller this year.*

"Let's go this way now, toward where the sun sets," Rusty said, a little less confidently.

As they walked, he saw a rock. "The rock! We're here!"

Gary Bear barreled down the hill right toward the rock, so excited to lay his paws on those berries. On his way down, his foot got caught in a hole, and he tumbled and rolled and rolled and tumbled right into … THE BRIAR PATCH.

Prickly, stickly, and not even one yummy berry. They knew they had gone the wrong way.

"That's a good look for you," Dave Deer called out to Gary Bear as Gary limped back up the hill, pulling prickers out of his thick fur.

Everyone looked at Rusty.

"Oh man, Rusty, this can't be right!!" huffed Gary Bear.

Rusty was embarrassed, but he tried to hide it. "No, no, I- we must have just taken a few wrong steps. I know the right way. Follow me!"

"I wish we had some acorns right now," Winston whined.

They found the top of another hill, where they could finally see the Red River.

"See, this is it!" Rusty said, sounding confident, but a bit uncertain in his heart. Out of the corner of his eye, he saw the grass rustle. Something was moving. *Maybe it's nothing.*

But then they heard the yips of a coyote, and Winston Squirrel said, "R-r-r-r-r-rusty, I think there's a coyote after us!"

AHHHH!

They all ran as fast as they could, down the hill, toward the white oak to hide. Winston started searching for acorns, but Gary quickly grabbed him. Rusty climbed the twisty tree to see if the coast was clear. Then he remembered.

"The twisted knot!" he exclaimed. "This is it. We're supposed to walk *this way*."

They didn't need any more encouragement to start running up the hill away from whatever was after them. When they got to the top of the hill, they looked down and saw the Red River. They turned toward the direction of the setting sun, which was getting a little lower in the sky now, and they started to run. They only had to find...

"THE ROCK!" they exclaimed. Not too big and not too small, and someone was sitting on it. It was Rusty's dad, with a big smile on his face.

"So, you finally found it, son?"

Rusty looked down, feeling a little silly.

"What, did you think I was going to let you have all the fun without me?" his dad asked. "And how about that 'coyote' you saw? *Yip-yip-yip*!"

"That was you?!" they all exclaimed.

Rusty's dad smiled, "You did a good job, Rusty. I'm proud of you."

"Well, I did lead Gary Bear into The Briar Patch," Rusty admitted.

His dad laughed, "Sometimes going the wrong way teaches you the right way. I am sure your feet will always remember the way now."

"What are we waiting for? Let's eat berries!" Winston called out. They laughed and followed him into The Sugar Bowl.

"You were right, Rusty, these are the best berries I've ever tasted," Gary Bear said with a mouth full of berries.

"I'm glad we didn't stop for any acorns," Winston agreed.

"Save some berries for the rest of us!" Dave added.

They picked as many berries as they could fit into their tummies and paws.

With berries in their bellies and adventure in their hearts, they set out for home.

And they let Rusty's dad lead the way.

ABOUT US

Ethan and Sherry Luhman currently live in Cedarburg, Wisconsin, after beginning their family in Missouri and New York. They have four children: Abram (7), Owain (5), Roman (2), and a baby girl on the way. Ethan is a pastor, and Sherry owns her own business, Oar + Arrow. When the "Safer at Home" mandate was put into place due to COVID-19, the Luhman family found themselves spending more time as a family, cuddled up together, reading more books and telling more stories. It turned out to be a time to put their dreams on paper and begin writing and painting the children's book they always dreamed of creating.

Ethan grew up on 60 acres in the rolling hills of southwestern Wisconsin, and he spent his summer days exploring, going on adventures with his brothers, and picking wild black raspberries. Sherry has been drawing animals since she could hold a pencil, and their children love animals and nature.

Beginning as bedtime stories, Ethan and Sherry created these characters to teach + encourage their children. Weaving together the beauty of nature, the importance of relationships, and the impact of a good adventure, they hope you find much joy reading *Rusty Raccoon and The Sugar Bowl*.

CPSIA information can be obtained
at www.ICGtesting.com
Printed in the USA
BVHW021950081120
592664BV00001B/3